The Battlefield Of Addiction

Author: Roland "Moe" Allen

The Battlefield of Addiction

I am dedicating this book to first & foremost God Almighty. He opened up the gates of addiction/hell & set me free. Also to my best friend Brandon Rawls, a.k.a. "Tubby", as well as so many loved ones that had their lives taken by the disease of addiction, and last but certainly not least, my Mother. She pretty much was the only one who did not give up or dispose of me, even with some of my family members trying to convince her to do so.

Table Of Content

What It Was Like 1

What Happened 8

What It Is Like Today 12

Addiction Is A Disease 15

Specifically For Those That Do Not Have The Disease 19

There Is Hope 25

PREFACE

For close to 20 years, I was very active in the disease of addiction. For the longest, I had absolutely no idea what was wrong with me. What started out as recreational smoking weed & drinking eventually turned into me using alcohol along with other narcotics. Then after some time of doing those things caused things to switch from recreational to maintenance. I knew I was not raised that way & I knew I was not a bad person. I simply didn't know what I didn't know. I lost my life caused by an overdose & it embedded some fear within me, but I was back doing the same thing less than a week later.

March 4th, 2014 is the day I decided to drop the shovel & stop digging my bottom. From that date forward, one day at a time, my rock bottom became the solid foundation on which my new life has been rebuilt upon. God has used me in so many ways to give back, doing service, to deliver what was so freely given. It has been a passion of mine for a while to write a book to share my story worldwide. Also, in this book, I'll be writing upon proper intellect & hope for many that are actively stuck in addiction to also deliver thorough knowledge for those that do not have the disease but may have a spouse, child, parent, etc. that does. To inform what avenues to take. As well as proper ways that's needed dealing with someone with the disease. To those that are trapped in addiction, there is most certainly a way out. March 4, 2020 will put me at 6 years of being truly sober, happy, joyous & free. Throughout my journey, I've lost more friends from the disease of addiction than I have my entire life. Of course, I do not save anybody but every day I do all I can to give back & help as many as possible to get sober & remain that way for the long haul, one day at a time.

WHAT IT WAS LIKE

I am from Baltimore, Maryland. I had an amazing childhood, as well as an amazing upbringing. My "sperm donor" as I call him was not in my life very often. So my main influences was my grandfather James "Boh" Cornish, my Uncle Rodney, a.k.a. "Mecca" & my grandmother remarried but I always considered him as my biological grandfather. His name was John, a.k.a. "Wes". Wes and my uncle were once in the military. My uncle was a Marine that fought in Desert Storm & Wes was a Navy SEAL. If anybody has ever seen the movie called "Men of Honor", my grandfather recently dealt with those times when racism was really at an all-time high & many white people did not want to serve with the black people. My uncle left to go into the Marine Corps when I was 6 months old. My uncle was the main one that taught me many things such as potty training, how to use condoms, things of that nature with both of my main influences being military men, they taught me that tough guy intellect as "men don't cry, vulnerability meant you were weak & don't rely on people. Any problems that you have, or things you may need, by any means necessary. My grandparents worked for General Motors & they both retired from there. They would get home around 2 or 3am with a bunch of friends they worked with & they would play cards & drink. So from an early age I figured that as long as your bills are paid, your responsibilities are taken care of, then you can do whatever you wants once all those things are taken care of. Pretty much like "work hard, play hard" type of deal.

I always made good grades in school. Made honor roll from elementary all the way up to I dropped out of school. I was also an athlete. I played football for many years & wrestled for a couple of years, but when I started ripping & running the streets & being active in addiction, all of that was put to the curb & lost its significance. I've also had a relationship with God since I was young. I freely went to church on my own for quite a few years, was baptized & all. Around the age of 14 years old, I started hustling. I liked big, fast money. My mother was not aware of what I was doing for the longest time. I would do chores around the house & she would give me an allowance but had no clue about the amount of money I truly had. I did those chores so that when I had all that money, if she were to catch me, I could tell her that I'd been saving my allowance money for a while. I had my first drunk around the age of 14 or 15 years old. Me & a bunch of friends went to a party; we brought a gallon of E & J brandy for the party & got our drink on. Me being in recovery, I've heard many speak upon their part of "what it was like" & a lot say that they drank to fit in, to feel comfortable in their own skin along with a select few of other reasons. But for myself, I never really cared to fit in. I've always known a lot of people & playing sports most certainly helps towards knowing people. One of the main reasons that I started drinking & using drugs was because from early on in my life, I was doing really well. I was making good grades, going to church, but was having a lot of the complete opposite come in return. So I figured that if I am doing what is right but so much keeps going wrong, let me try another route. Not much longer after drinking, I started smoking marijuana. Due to dumb decisions of mine, I dropped out of high school. But many years later, I went & got my G.E.D. I've heard some say how "they're a product of their environments" but that is not true. That everyone is "products of the decisions we choose to make." Throughout life, we make choices, but in the end our choices make us. So due to me hustling, consequences started taking place. I've been on probation. I've done time in jail, but none of that was enough to make me want to do different.

The longer that I travel along upon my recovery journey, I tend to do a lot of hindsight. Which helps me remember where I came from, how far I've come along & how much I've changed. Also, by me doing that allows me to see where God played a lot of parts in my life that I was not able to see back then. Around the age of 17, being very close to 18, God made it known to me that I ought to try implementing some discipline in my life. Anytime that I was in school, playing sports, locked up or institutionalized I was your top modeled citizen. I had no problem with following rules & guidelines. But as soon as I would get released, free will came back & I did what I wanted to do again. So the alternatives that came upon me was to either join the military or get into boxing. So my choice was boxing which I absolutely loved when being active in that, doing training you cannot be out using & partying a lot like I was, so all of that slowed down a lot. About 3 ½ years into it, I hurt my wrist very severely. The doctor said that if any kind of injury to that wrist happened again, I ran a high risk of losing proper usage of my right hand & go figure that is my dominant/writing hand. So I made a decision to stop fighting & due to that injury I was also introduced to opiates, a.k.a. Percocet. Another huge reason that I loved using is because I do not like to feel. If it is not happy, joyous, or freeing I do not like having to feel the opposite emotions. My mother met a man through her best friend & he happened to be from Youngstown, Ohio. When they got deeper involved, she wanted me to move to Ohio, he was wanting to move to Maryland. So they ended up moving to Ohio, they got married. He bought them a home & Ohio is where they settled. Up to that point, I never even heard of Ohio. After a few years of them living here, I'd gotten the idea of moving there. Trying to get a fresh start, going there where I did not know anyone & try to stop doing all the crazy stuff that I was in my hometown. But of course, I did not know this until I got into recovery is, you take yourself wherever you go at. Making that move like I did is what recovery calls a "geographical cure". It was not very long until I found people that were a lot like me & that was into the very same things that I called myself trying to get away from.

Here in Akron, Ohio they have a detox center called ADM. I'd been in that facility 7 times. Each time that I went, I really had the motive & intentions of staying sober. But of course, I was going to buck the system & do things my way, rather than follow the suggestions they deliver. In one of my consequences I had prior to coming to Ohio, they gave me 2 options which was either to go do the jail time that followed my charge or go to treatment. They had something new going on in drug courts which was called "85-07". I was pulled over one night & had a little over half of an ounce of marijuana that was individually bagged up inside of a sandwich bag. That was a part of what I was hustling at the time. They were trying to charge me with "intent to distribute", which is a felony charge. But I lied & told them that it was for my personal use only & that is how it was when I purchased it. By God's grace, I do not have any felonies on my record but should have had many of them. So I went to a treatment facility that's located in West Baltimore called Gaudenzia. It was an all-male facility & was a 6 month program. I'd never been to treatment up to that point & had no idea what I was going into. I went "cold turkey" while being in there. Meaning I was withdrawing from opiates & alcohol without any assistance from medication they give to help people not have severe symptoms from withdrawing. I completed that program in 4 ½ months. Never had any dirty urines, never came late back on passes. I stayed sober for a year & a half, very close to 2 years & my grandmother, which was my best friend, my whole world died from lung cancer & from going through that, I chose to go back to using. I am unable to put into words what my grandmother meant to me. Having to watch her wither away day by day from lung cancer is by far the hardest thing till this very day that I've had to deal with.

So each time that I would get released from ADM detox center, I'd stay sober for a few months, a couple of weeks. Each time my stint from not using got less & less. But my last time in there, something was different. I could feel that difference but could not put a name to it. Even some of the employees were saying the same exact thing. After coming into recovery I learned what that difference was. God embedded in me what is called "the gift of desperation". God had made it known to me that I kept trying to run the show & do things my way & it was never successful & that I needed to follow those suggestions that they deliver. All throughout the day people that are in recovery & have at least a year or more sober come to speak. Delivering their experiences, strength & hope. Out of all of those that would come there were 3 specific ones that I'd always gravitate to the most. When I was released that last time, all of these feelings & emotions that I'd been numbing for years started hitting me like a whirlwind. I knew for sure that I did not want to go get alcohol or drugs to Novocain those emotions like I normally would do. So I swallowed my pride & followed the suggestion of picking up the phone to call those numbers of those 3 guys that I gravitated to. I called the one individual & did not get an answer, so rather than lose hope, I called the 2nd person. He picked up the phone & we talked for a good 15/20 minutes. Then that first number I called that did not answer called back. He picked me up on what is known as a "12-step call". He came to pick me up, took me to a bonfire around a bunch of people that were sober. The following morning he came to pick me up again & took me out to this inpatient facility center called IBH and got me a Big Book. We sat there under the pavilion & he began taking me through the 12 steps. He not much longer became my sponsor & I've been doing the deal, staying sober ever since.

WHAT HAPPENED

As I said in the previous chapter, I'd been using drugs & alcohol to the point that I had eventually crossed the "imaginary line" recovery calls it. When that line was crossed, I had lost the choice as if I were going to drink or drug or not. It became necessary for me to drink &/or put drugs in me in order to function & not be sick. For the longest, alcohol & drugs were not my problem, they were my solution. That is how I dealt with life on life's terms. But it came to a point & time where my solution no longer filled its purpose. When my sponsor & I started reading the Big Book, it was like an epiphany. I'd come to learn so much that I was not aware of. I'd come to learn that addiction "IS" a disease. That what makes "real" alcoholic/addicts different than the so-called "normal" is whenever we put drugs &/or alcohol in us, it becomes our higher power. It takes all control of us & tells us what to do. Alcoholic/addicts have a 3-sided disease. They have what is called "the mental obsession, the spiritual malady & the phenomenon of craving". Which is why the saying goes that "one is too many & one thousand is not enough". When those who have the disease of addiction, all they want & all that matters is more & more. Then they're trying to fill "a hole in the soul" a.k.a. a spiritual malady/sickness which can only be contained by God. And anytime that they're not drinking or drugging, that is all they are able to think about. I've learned how & why I'm powerless over alcohol & drugs & that everyday I have to stay tapped into my Higher Power which can solve all of my problems.

Those first 6 times of me going in & out of detox, I would do things like isolate, try locking myself in my house. But even with having a few months, weeks, or days of just not using, that urge was still there, my mind would dwell upon using & it would eventually overpower me & next thing you know I am using again because whatever controls your mind, controls you.

I read & learned about how only God has the ability to have freed me from my alcoholism. There is "No" chemical solution to/for a spiritual malady/problem. The way that He set me free was by me honestly & thoroughly working all the 12 steps. Faith without works is dead. All 12 step programs are spiritual a.k.a. the complete opposite of religion. There are so many, even those that have the disease of addiction, that fail to realize that drugs & alcohol are only but "symptoms" of the problem. The "actual" problem is the mind. After I worked the 12 steps as well as actually being in recovery, I was about 6 months sober & I am getting myself ready to go to work, doing my spiritual readings & meditation & God made it known to me that my mental obsession had been lifted. Anytime that I would get upset, wanna celebrate, or whatever, no longer did I think about using or had to fight/struggle with the temptation of using dominating my brain. That to me is absolutely mind-blowing to say the very least. In 12 step literature & other readings it is known & especially proven that nobody in human form has the ability or power to take the mental obsession away from those inflicted with the disease of addiction. The same exact way that some people have sugar diabetes must take insulin, the same exact way that cancer patients have to do chemotherapy, those that have the disease of addiction have alternatives as well. But it is not forced upon them, they have a choice. But the treatment for those with the disease are suggested to go to meetings, to get a sponsor that has a working knowledge of the steps, get a Higher Power, get active in recovery. This is my first time ever being involved in a 12-step program/fellowship & the evidence is official. This is the longest amount of time that I have ever been sober. March 4th, 2020 I had 6 years sober. Everything that recovery lets be known has blossomed & happened for me plus a whole bunch more. I've also been blessed to see recovery change many other people's lives in so many fascinating ways. But it does take work. A lot more has to be done than just not using. There are some in recovery that are only abstinent but do not work the steps, do not have a relationship with a Higher Power, do not indulge in service work & they have a couple of years, but they're absolutely miserable. It is not hard at all to tell those who put the work in & who does not in recovery. I was miserable enough during many years of being stuck in addiction, I refuse to be that way sober. And without a doubt, many of those in recovery that do not put the work in eventually start using again & a lot of them never make it back because the disease of addiction snatched their lives away. I have lost & known more people that have died being active in addiction than I have my entire life & I am 34 years old. So for myself, every day I am putting in work towards my recovery. I had my life taken away from the disease but God seen fit to spare mine. The disease is truly life or death & only guarantees 3 things which is jails, institutions or death.

WHAT IT IS LIKE TODAY

I recently was blessed to celebrate my 6 year sobriety anniversary. Unlike most, I never had that "pink cloud" effect. Which is some get sober & everything is just grandiose, they quickly get the girlfriend or boyfriend back & everything is peaches & cream. I fight hard & put massive work in on the daily to have obtained the time that I am blessed with. Nobody said that life was going to be easy. Nothing that's truly worth it in life never does come to be easy but it is surely always worth it. The same exact way that I put work in to destruct myself & my life being active in addiction, I flipped it & put that effort into reconstructing myself & my life. As I said before, real recovery is much more than only just not drinking or drugging. Of course not using is vital, but for myself I have to put work into bettering myself from the inside. There are some that believe it's okay to live corrupt on the daily, but just as long as they do not pick up & use then that is all that matters. I am the complete opposite way. It is not okay for me to display the corrupt, grimey behaviors that I did while using in sobriety. I tend to compete with myself rather than compete with others. I work on trying to be a better man than I was the day before. By me doing that, I am also very cautious of the people I surround myself with. The truth of the matter is that you're only as good as who & what you surround yourself with. It is truly vital to have those around you that have the same intentions & motives that you have. By me trying to keep getting better does not mean that I never make mistakes. But I learn & profit from those mistakes rather than repeat them. A mistake is only made once, anything after that is a choice. I am not who I used to be when I began my recovery journey. I am not fully where I want to be either, but I sure as hell am glad that I am not who & what I used to be.

Throughout my journey thus far I've obtained good jobs & lost a couple of jobs. I've dealt with a lot of severe hurt & heartbreak; I've had some spread lies & rumors on me. Some that I considered good friends & support that stabbed me right in my back. But I've also had some amazing times & experiences. You tend to appreciate joy when you have dealt with a lot of pain. You tend to cherish happiness when you have had a lot of sorrow & disappointments. There were a lot of things in life before getting sober that my go-to was to handle with getting drunk and/or high. So now being on the recovery journey, all of those hurtful, disappointing & mournful situations come back around so that I can learn to get through & deal with them properly. I do not deliver fairytales to people. A lot of times when some speak about recovery, they want to only mention the good things & hold back on letting the flip side be known. I guess feeling that speaking on the hardships will chase or discourage some from not wanting to get sober & give recovery a chance. Without a doubt, sobriety & recovery are amazing gifts & blessings from God, but it is not always peaches & cream. Sometimes the best part of my day is going through hardships without having to use in order to make it through them. In sobriety, just as long as you don't pick up you have a chance. Picking up and using does not make your problems go away.

Doing so actually makes things worse because not only is whatever itself is a massive struggle in itself. I have seen people go back to using over success, as well as failures. As I've been properly taught, step one is the only step that has to be done 100 percent. If step one is not properly done, then the rest will not do any good. Step one is "We admitted we were powerless over drugs/alcohol, that our lives had become unmanageable". I had also spoke upon previously that I've always had a relationship with God. But when my grandmother died it caused me to build up spiritual prejudices & I stopped turning my will & my life over to Him, which are my thoughts & my actions. It is not very hard to tell when doing hindsight, that once I stopped praying & asking God to guide me, my life went downhill more & more. So when I got involved with the recovery process & after working those steps to get set free from so much that was blocking me off from God & freely allow Him to manage my life again, it continues to keep getting better than when I was the one running things without Him. I am powerless, lack of power was my dilemma – so every day I freely allow God to utilize His power within me & for Him to control my thoughts & actions & be the manager of me & my life.

ADDICTION IS A DISEASE

There are many out here that believe that addiction is not a disease. There are many who are unaware of addiction being a disease. There are many that are actually killing those who have the disease by telling them things like "they're weak, that all they need is will power, etc.". For those that do not have the disease try going to the store & take a bunch of Ex-Lax & when they start to take effect, use your will power to "hold your poop in" and refrain from not using the bathroom & see where it gets you. The exact same way that your willpower cannot stop or hold back the force of what the medication is doing, well that is the same ordeal with those who have the disease. A lot tend to have sympathy for a loved one that has cancer but treat those that have the disease of addiction the complete opposite. Those who do not have the disease can go to the bar, have a beer or 2 & go home & that'll be the end of it. But the "real alcoholic" goes to the bar, has a beer & sets off the phenomenon of craving & will not stop until they either black out or pass out. Those that do not have the disease may deal with a family member or loved one that does & they say things such as "why can't you just stop or stay stopped, or stop being weak & boost up your willpower."

Doing things as such actually aggravates them & causes them to drink or drug that much more. I know for myself, coming up I surely never said, when I grow up, I want to be a person that uses all day, every day to feed an addiction. Many others that I come across in recovery did not have it in their life plans to be afflicted with the disease. When being stuck & active in addiction, we have to drink &/or drug to be "normal". Those who may not have it say things like "well they can choose to say no & not do it" which is true. But once they're to that point, to not use means that they'll feel like absolute death & garbage all day & all night. For those that are "normal", imagine having the flu, or pneumonia & intensify it by 75 percent. Imagine having to feel that all day, every day. I am sure that you're going to go to the store to get some cold meds & utilize other remedies to not feel that all day, every day. That is what it is like for those who are wrapped up in active using. For those who only drink alcohol &/or liquor, they can literally die from withdrawal/not having alcohol to put in them. Then of course, there are those who do not have the disease that say "well, nobody told them to get themselves to that point." Well again as I said, a lot did not plan or expect to get to that point. As crazy as it may sound, or regardless of what some may think, those afflicted with the disease, especially early on, they a lot of times cannot remember when getting to that point either. Reason being is because they did not have their first drunk or high & were instantly stuck in addiction. It was built up over time. Early on when many had their first drunk, they had the choice of not drinking again for a while. They may have gotten too drunk & were hugging the toilet swearing they would never do it again. But after they get fully back together, they get that thought of "they can't wait to do it again".

Why do some end up getting the disease & some do not? Who knows really. Why did racism come about, why do some grow up to be psycho killers? It is one of those things that just happens. My mother was not big at all when it came to drinking or using drugs. She can drink a couple wine coolers one time at a family gathering & not touch another drink for a year or more. Alcohol does not affect her the way it does me. But addiction does run in my family. There are those who do not believe that addiction is hereditary. I beg to differ. If there were uncles, aunts, grandparents, etc. that had the disease, it should not be a shock that one of the uncles has 3 kids, at least one runs a very high chance of having the disease of addiction. Those that have the disease, if they run through their family members, it will be a couple that had it also prior to them being born. The disease is also progressive. What that means is even though I have 6 years sober, if I started drinking & using things will get worse instantly as if I never stopped. I have experienced it myself & I've known people in recovery that have had 10, 15, 20 years & thought that because they've been sober all of that time, that they can drink like a "normal person" & before they know it, they were back drinking cases, gallons, etc. of beer or liquor. Which is why the saying goes, "once an alcoholic/addict, always an alcoholic/addict." I am very much aware that I can't drink or drug moderately. I would not even attempt to just have one beer. I like to get drunk &/or high to the max & I am okay with that. I enjoy the sober life!

18

SPECIFICALLY FOR THOSE THAT DO NOT HAVE THE DISEASE

Unfortunately, addiction continues to rise stronger & stronger. There are many that are not properly informed about addiction & ways to deal with loved ones that are. Knowledge truly is power. It is never easy watching & knowing a child, spouse, sister, brother, etc. being actively stuck in addiction. I've witnessed those that have a loved one stuck in addiction love those individuals literally to death. How that happens is because of those watching & knowing their loved ones are actively using & let's say Larry's the one actively using & his mother gives him everything he demands. He comes to her asking for money & she struggles with saying no because it makes her feel bad so she gives him money and he goes to get a bag of heroin which causes him to overdose & die. Or Brandon comes home drunk, demanding money. He starts breaking things around the house until his wife gives him either money &/or car keys so she breaks & gives him what he wants & on his way to the store, he wrecks the car & kills the person involved in the crash. And a lot of times when people stuck in addiction are aware that they have a wife, brother, mother, etc. that easily gives in, they actually feed upon that & by those people always giving in, it becomes what is called "enabling". And those with big/soft hearts feel guilty or ashamed by saying no & they think that they're helping them. To those reading this that feel those ways, you're not helping them at all.

When it comes to dealing with loved ones that are actively feeding their addictions, there are two actions that are vital & that is tough love & loving them from a distance, or detachment. I know from experience that my mother at a point & time was the kind that would feel bad about not giving me help or money when I was down & out. Even though she never gave up on me, even though many of my family and her friends kept telling her to kick me to the curb, she never did. She kept praying for me & believing that God was going to bring good out of my addiction. But by her delivering me tough love put me into survival mode, sink or swim mode. She had told me that either I get myself together, or I could continue to keep using but I had to get from under her roof. I am sure it was hard and hurtful for her to do that, but that played a part in me taking action towards getting myself together.

During one of my times of using, I actually overdosed in my mother's home. She was supposed to work that day, but did not go. If she would have went to work, I would not be alive. If the girl I was with decided just to walk & leave as if nothing happened, I would not be alive. My mother & her boyfriend had to prop me under their arms, drag me down a bunch of steps. She's telling my sister to call 9-1-1 & my sister is panicking & all upset because her big brother is laying on the floor dead. My mom is trying to calm her down while giving me C.P.R. She was able to get me to come to right as the ambulance pulled up. The paramedics get me into the truck & hit me with Narcan. My mother did not know I was alive for an hour & a half, when I called home from the hospital. 20 dollars took my life. My mother had no idea that I was using to the extent that I was until that point.

As humans, we're equipped to go in fight or flight mode when we're either in danger, or when we're in tough spots or situations. For those who do, or may not, there is so much power in prayer. Even though it took a good, long while before I got sober, there were all kinds of crazy things that I did running the streets, that could have caused me to lose my life. I put myself in dangerous situations many times and without a doubt, I know that the reason that I was OK is because my mother is a prayer warrior & she sent prayer requests worldwide, having many people in different states praying for me. It is also important to pray over yourselves, for God to give you the strength to be able to deliver that tough love. To help you to stay strong during these times of your loved ones being out there with you being aware of it & it causing you hurt & sorrow.

Addiction is a family disease. Even though one person may be using, the family suffers because of it & it takes effect upon the family & loved ones. A lot of parents tend to beat themselves up when they have children actively using, or wondering what they did or did not do. I mean it is not unheard of that there are some parents that partied with their kids. But me going through what I did throughout my time using has absolutely nothing to do with my upbringing & actually a lot of my upbringing played a huge role into why I did not do a lot of the crazy things that I've heard & known others to do. Regardless, we're all taught right from wrong & it's up to each individual in which route they choose to take. Many times when people indulge & drink &/or use to the point of addiction, nobody put a gun to their heads & force them to do so. Even if someone did put a gun to their heads, they still have the choice to say no. I am sure for a lot, it may be easier said than done to not balance themselves, but I assure those that struggle with doing so, please do not.

They also have what is called "Al-Anon", which is a fellowship of men & women that have loved ones afflicted with the disease. It allows them to build support to help deal & get through the journey of your loved ones being actively stuck in addiction. It helps a lot to know that you're not alone & that you're not the only one going through it. As the saying goes & is very much true when they say "it's power in numbers". If you're not aware of Al-Anon or have no idea as of where to begin to look, simply Google Al-Anon meetings in your area.

Something else that I've witnessed loved ones do for those actively stuck in addiction is anytime they get into trouble they instantly run to their rescue, trying to do all they can to get their loved ones out of trouble, or to lessen their troubles as much as possible, which is not good to do. When they start getting into legal troubles, allow them to deal with those consequences. Pain can be a great motivator. Always coming to their rescue simply causes them to do more & more crazy things, thinking that you're always going to come & bail them out of whatever they may do. One of the hardest things about being a bystander & watching loved ones out using is because you never know what the outcome is going to be. It is never known as if they're going to eventually get sober, or if they're going to die, etc. All that can be done is to place them in the hands of God, keep them uplifted in prayer & as hard as it can be, just let them go through. Trying to control them &/or the situation will drive you completely insane.

Early on when I got sober, I used to despise myself & things that I've done. But through more time, I know that all that I've been through has formed me into who & what I am now. God turned my mess of a life into a powerful message. He has used the worst of me & times to mold me to continue to keep getting better. I know it is hard & hurtful seeing those you care about going through it & while dealing with it. It's hard to think or believe greatness is being formed at times, but I am a living witness & testimony of God's handiwork. One of the hardest things for those who do not have the disease of addiction is that no matter how supportive someone may be, no matter how much care they have, it is one of those things that cannot or will not be able to ever be fully understood. But it is what makes those who have it be so close & understanding with others that do. I've been able to be so helpful to those that have this disease that others that do not have it but may be doctors, psychiatrists, counselors were not able to reach.

Even with me having it but being on the other side, I truly hate how the disease of addiction has taken so many lives of people that I know, or even people that I did not know. I not that long ago had my best friend that I considered a brother have his life taken by heroin. Besides losing my grandmother, I must say losing him was the second hardest thing I've had to deal with. Me being in recovery & trying to help so many & see so many die takes a toll. So I know how it feels. I am not coming from a position that I have not had experience. I deal with it on a daily.

THERE IS HOPE

For the longest time, I had absolutely no idea what was going on with me. I was completely unaware as of to why I eventually had no control over whether or not I was going to use. I could not even remember when that whole transition took place. It started getting to the point to where committing suicide was getting more & more welcoming & I am surely not even the kind of person that ever was suicidal. I never could pull myself to put a gun to my head & pull the trigger, but I would plan different scenarios such as stand on the sidewalk & wait for a bus, or big truck to come down the street in full stride & just step off the curb so that the driver would not have the opportunity to hit the brakes or swerve to avoid hitting me. One of the main thoughts that always came across my mind was thinking about the mother of my Godson having to tell him that I died. I still get choked up when I think about it. There was a few years during my addiction that I was in a really dark place mentally & spiritually. I was what I call the "walking dead". I was here in the physical, but was completely dead inside. There was not anything that was scaring me at all. The most that someone could do was kill me & that is what I was wanting.

It was not until I came into recovery & started reading the Big Book, that it has impacted & changed myself & made my life so much better. The book was written many years ago, but it was as if someone was a mind reader & wrote a book all about me without knowing who I was. It described me to the tee. All the ways I felt, why I did the things that I did. Which is why the saying is absolutely true, "knowledge is power". In recovery, I tend to hear some complain about having to go to meetings, along with other things that is suggested. Those that have the disease, when we're out there feeding our addiction, we go to any lengths plus more to get what we want & need. When being out there, we freely partake in destructing ourselves without second guessing, but you have those that want to complain & buck the system when it comes to putting forth work in recovery. If you take half of the energy that was put feeding that addiction, you will do just fine in recovery. When you work for something as opposed to just have it freely given you tend to cherish it much more.

For those that are still actively using, I mean this from the bottom of my heart: you do not have to live that way anymore. These days along with being in recovery, I truly live these days. Before being out there I was not living. I was simply just existing. Of course at a point & time drinking & all of that was fun but eventually came to a point & time that I had to put something in me just to be normal to do the day-to-day regular life. I was incarcerated in the worst prison to be in, which is your own mind when it is working against you. I've done jail time, but I've also been locked up without bars & steel doors holding me in a cell. I always tell a lot that are new to recovery to give the fellowship/program 6 months of applying the suggestions & if by that 6-month mark, they are not satisfied, they can easily be refunded that misery of being a slave to addiction. I am very straightforward when it comes to recovery because it is not a joke at all. They are not lying to you at all. Change can be scary, but it is so worth it getting sober & being given another life & chance. The grass most certainly is greener on the other side.

I do a lot plus more in recovery, consistently trying to give back what was so freely given & this here book is one of my ways of me doing that. I poured my heart & soul in this book in hopes that it helps so many, especially those stuck in addiction. Even if it only were to help one person, I am okay with that. I know that there are those stuck in addiction that have children, grandchildren, parents, significant others that love them dearly & do not want to lose their grandparents, mother, father, husband, wife, etc. from addiction taking them away. Even though it has to be done for self in order for long-term sobriety to partake, you're able to use spouses, kids, grandkids, etc. as motivation. If there may be those out there in addiction that may not love or care about themselves, just know that I do & I mean that with my whole heart. You do not have to personally know someone to care about them. Just by us having the disease ties us together automatically.

When you come into recovery, that will instantly give you an extended, huge family because all over the world there are many in recovery & they all are your family regardless of knowing them. I've been to church before, retreats & met many people. But I have never experienced so much real, true love, bonds & relationships as I have in recovery. I always make it a point to put in prayer requests asking many to pray for those out there still sick & suffering, as well as for the children that have no say in the matter. I really do hope that this book gets placed in the right hands to help many, I really do. To those that purchase this book & take time to read it, I truly want to thank you. If nobody has told you that they love you, I do.

www.ingramcontent.com/pod-product-compliance
Lightning Source LLC
Chambersburg PA
CBHW050818160726
48004CB00002B/896